This Walker book belongs to:

_____

_____

_____

First published 1985, 1988 and 2004 in *When We Went to the Park*,
Out and About and *Olly and Me* by Walker Books Ltd
87 Vauxhall Walk, London SE11 5HJ

This edition published 2016

2 4 6 8 10 9 7 5 3 1

This book has been typeset in Plantin Light Educational

Printed in China

British Library Cataloguing in Publication Data:
a catalogue record for this book is available from the British Library

ISBN 978-1-4063-7283-0

www.walker.co.uk

THE NURSERY
COLLECTION
AUTUMN

Shirley Hughes

WALKER BOOKS
AND SUBSIDIARIES
LONDON · BOSTON · SYDNEY · AUCKLAND

People in the Pond

Peering over the stone rim,
we see four faces looking back at us:
Buster, Mum, Olly and me,
wobbly and green in the water.
Down below, the fish glide,
grey and silver,
pink and gold;
hovering, rising,
then suddenly diving,
with a brisk whisk of their tails,
while the little fish slip in and out like ripples.
Now our faces break up into bits of watery light.
But the boy in the middle of the pond
stands still as stone,
endlessly pouring water from his stone jar.

Misty

Mist in the morning,
Raw and nippy,
Leaves on the pavement,
Wet and slippy.
Sun on fire
Behind the trees,
Muddy boots,
Muddy knees.

Shop windows,
Lighted early,
Soaking grass,
Dewy, pearly.
Red, lemon,
Orange and brown,
Silently, softly,
The leaves float down.

Wind

I like the wind.
The soft, summery, gentle kind,
The gusty, blustery, fierce kind.
Ballooning out the curtains,
Blowing things about,
Wild and wilful everywhere.
I *do* like the wind.

When we went to the park we saw
birds swooping in the sky,

and so many leaves that I
couldn't count them all.

Feasts

Apples heaped on market barrows,
Juicy plums and stripy marrows.

Grains of barley,
Carefully stored.

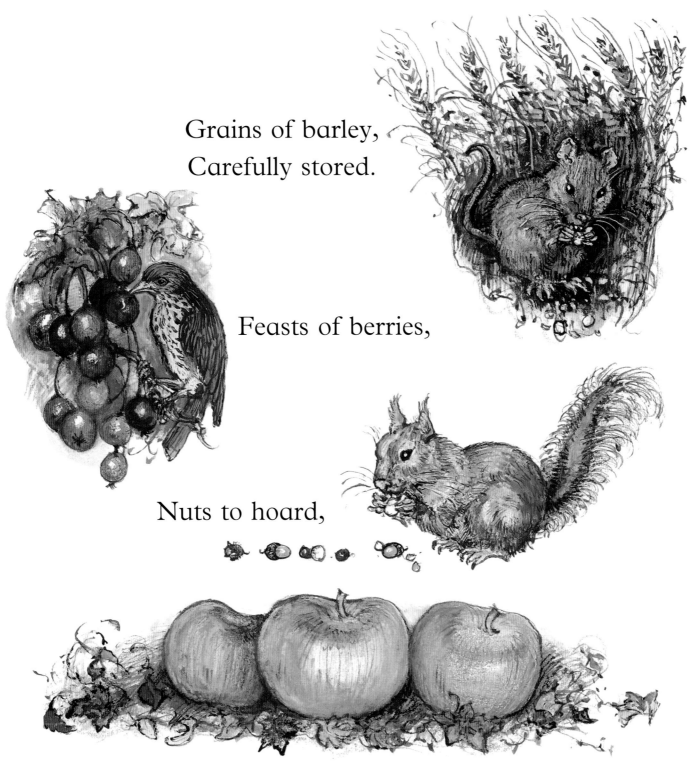

Feasts of berries,

Nuts to hoard,

And ripe pumpkins, yellow and green,
To light with candles at Hallowe'en.

Fire

Fire is a dragon
(Better beware),
Dangerous and beautiful
(Better take care).
Puffing out smoke
As soon as it's lit,
Licking up leaves,
Crackle and spit!

Sending up sparks
Into the sky
That hover a moment
And suddenly die.
Fire is a dragon,
Alive in the night;
Fiery dragon,
Glittering bright.

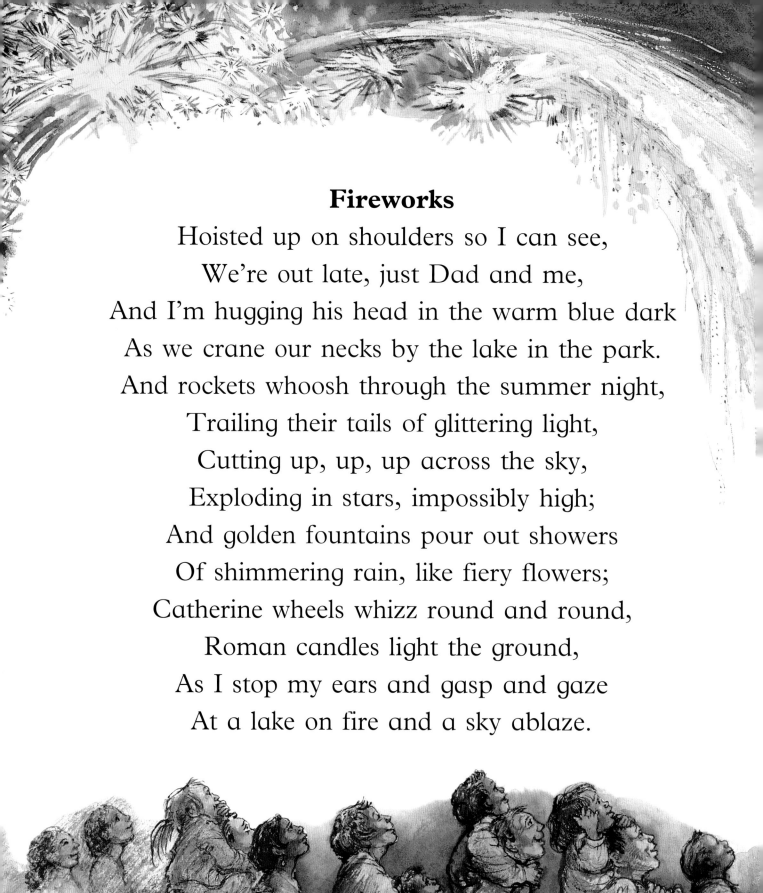

Fireworks

Hoisted up on shoulders so I can see,
We're out late, just Dad and me,
And I'm hugging his head in the warm blue dark
As we crane our necks by the lake in the park.
And rockets whoosh through the summer night,
Trailing their tails of glittering light,
Cutting up, up, up across the sky,
Exploding in stars, impossibly high;
And golden fountains pour out showers
Of shimmering rain, like fiery flowers;
Catherine wheels whizz round and round,
Roman candles light the ground,
As I stop my ears and gasp and gaze
At a lake on fire and a sky ablaze.

Do John, mo leathbhádóir, mo chara, mo chéile – Muireann
Do Joke, a thuigeann an tábhacht atá le teidí deas – Paddy

Foilsithe den chéad uair in 2019, faoi chlúdach crua, ag Futa Fata, An Spidéal, Co. na Gaillimhe, Éire

An dara cló, faoi chlúdach bog © 2021 Futa Fata

An téacs © 2019–2021 Muireann Ní Chíobháin

Maisiú © 2019–2021 Paddy Donnelly

Tá Futa Fata buíoch d'Fhoras na Gaeilge faoin tacaíocht airgid.

Foras na Gaeilge

Thacaigh An Chomhairle Ealaíon le forbairt an leabhair seo faoina scéim
Maoiniú Deontais do na hEalaíona

ISBN: 978-1-910945-81-0